SPOTLIGHT ON EXPLORERS AND COLONIZATION™

SAMUEL DE CHAMPLAIN

Founder of New France and Quebec City

ANDREW VIETZE

ROSEN PUBLISHING
New York

Published in 2017 by The Rosen Publishing Group, Inc.
29 East 21st Street, New York, NY 10010

First Edition

Library of Congress Cataloging-in-Publication Data

Names: Vietze, Andrew, author.
Title: Samuel de Champlain: Founder of New France and Quebec City / Andrew Vietze.
Description: First edition. | New York : Rosen Publishing, 2017. | Series:
Spotlight on explorers and colonization | Includes bibliographical
references and index.
Identifiers: LCCN 2016018732| ISBN 9781508172307 (library bound) | ISBN
9781508172277 (pbk.) | ISBN 9781508172284 (6-pack)
Subjects: LCSH: Champlain, Samuel de, 1574–1635. | New France—Discovery and
exploration. | Explorers—North America—Biography. |Explorers—France—Biography.
Classification: LCC F1030.1 .V54 2016 | DDC 910.92 [B] —dc23
LC record available at https://lccn.loc.gov/2016018732

Manufactured in China

CONTENTS

FATHER OF NEW FRANCE

As a boy, Samuel de Champlain could often be found on the docks of his hometown of Brouage, France. He loved the sea, and tales of an unexplored continent across the salty Atlantic captivated him. Champlain grew up to become a master mariner. He made at least twenty-seven crossings of the Atlantic to explore that exciting new land. And he did it without ever losing a ship. He ventured into parts of North America no European had ever been before and grew famous as a mapmaker and adventurer. But he was much more than

Among the most famous French explorers, Samuel de Champlain helped France expand its empire into North America.

that. Samuel de Champlain was a soldier, a spy, a writer, an artist, a diplomat, and a humanist. Today, his name is honored by one of the nation's most important lakes and many mountains, colleges, towns, and cities. Several nations celebrated him. He'll always be remembered as the founder of Quebec City and the Father of New France.

A BOY AND HIS MAPS

Samuel de Champlain was all but born to the sea. He came into the world near the Bay of Biscay in 1567. His father, Antoine Champlain, made his living on ships as a captain in the French navy. Little is known about his mother, Marguerite Le Roy. Some historians believe she also came from a family of fishermen. Where Samuel went to school is uncertain. It's clear, though, that he learned to sail, draw, and make maps at a young age. He also mastered the arts of war—shooting, swordplay, and riding. Champlain learned seamanship from his

A brave adventurer with a love of the sea, Samuel de Champlain was the first European to explore and map many places in the Great Lakes area of North America.

father. They sailed together often when Antoine left on business. When speaking to the queen regent about the art of navigation, Champlain said, "[It] won my love at a very early age, and inspired me to venture nearly all of my life on the turbulent waves of the ocean."

THE WORLD AS THEY KNEW IT

Seventy years had passed since Columbus "discovered" a vast continent to the west. Europeans had still not found a northwestern sea route to Asia despite centuries of searching. By the late 1500s, the Spanish had expanded their empire into Mexico, Florida, and the Caribbean. The English had explored much of the northeast of North America. France had made many attempts to colonize the coast of what is now Canada. Magellan's crew had even circled the globe. But no one had ever been able to sail northwest to reach the riches of

The 1492 visit of Christopher Columbus to North America changed the way Europeans thought about their world, inspiring millions and beginning a new age of exploration.

India and China. Surely there was a way to sail through North America to the Pacific! It seemed to be just waiting there to be found. Every European nation wanted to be the first to discover it. All of this was heady stuff for a young boy with salt in his veins and maps in his mind.

JACQUES CARTIER

The young Champlain keenly studied the journeys of others. He especially liked explorer Jacques Cartier, who was the first to claim North America for the French. In 1534, Cartier made a high-speed crossing of the Atlantic. He reached Newfoundland just three weeks after setting sail from France. As he journeyed up the St. Lawrence River, he kidnapped some Iroquois natives he found there. He brought them back to France with him. Cartier made the trip again the next year. This time he went further down the river to a site near today's Montreal. There he set up a fort.

Samuel de Champlain was fascinated by the travels of his countryman, Jacques Cartier, who visited North America more than sixty years before him.

Many of his men died, and relations with the Iroquois worsened quickly. Later French settlers worked to live in harmony with the Native Americans. But Cartier was never kind or patient with the native people he met. The explorer made several attempts at colonizing this land. He failed each time due to poor planning, scurvy, and conflict with the native people.

CHAMPLAIN SEES THE NEW WORLD

In 1599, Champlain got to visit the New World for himself. Desperately curious about America, he was invited along on a trip with his uncle, a seaman and something of a French legend. They spent months island-hopping in the Caribbean. They also visited Spanish ports in Mexico, Panama, and Colombia on a trade mission. Champlain secretly gathered information about Spanish ways and holdings in the New World, "of which no Frenchman had been able to gain knowledge," as he put it. And he openly studied the best methods to navigate and

In 1598, the young Samuel de Champlain visited the Caribbean with his uncle, spending months exploring, making maps, and spying on the Spanish.

cross the Atlantic. Some say it was the French explorer who first came up with the idea to connect the Pacific and the Atlantic by making a canal across Panama. King Henry IV of France so appreciated the intelligence that Champlain gathered on this trip that he gave him a pension and made him a noble.

GEOGRAPHER TO THE KING

In 1601, Champlain was called to the court of King Henry IV of France. There, the king offered him the job of royal geographer. While working for the king, he talked to fishermen. They had chased cod to the northern shores of North America. Champlain's interest was piqued. In March 1603, he traveled to North America himself at last. He went with Captain François Gravé Du Pont as part of a fur-trading expedition. The ship docked at the trading post Tadoussac on May 26. Next, the explorer made his first journey down the St. Lawrence and Saguenay Rivers,

The French built their first trading post in the New World in 1600 at Tadoussac, near the Saguenay Fjord on the St. Lawrence River, in what is now Quebec, Canada.

looking for a way to Asia. He befriended the Montagnais people and promised to help them defeat their enemies, the Iroquois. They told him of a great sea to the west. He thought they were referring to the Northwest Passage. But they were certainly describing the Great Lakes.

THE SAVAGES

Upon his return to France later that year, Champlain published an account of his travels called *Des Sauvages*. It inspired King Henry IV to consider colonizing North America. They shared a dream of a peaceful, prosperous New France. The king sent Champlain back across the Atlantic in 1604. This time he was to look into building a permanent settlement. Champlain was the geographer on an expedition led by Pierre Dugua, Sieur de Mons. The group decided to build their colony on an island. It was located at the mouth of the St. Croix River, between what's now Maine and New Brunswick,

King Henry IV of France was a personal friend of Samuel de Champlain's, and, like the explorer, he dreamed of many prosperous French colonies in North America.

Canada. The colonists arrived late in the season and began constructing villages. Problems arose right away. The island had poor soil and little freshwater. Harsh winds blew from the sea. A brutal winter claimed the lives of almost half of the colonists. They abandoned the effort soon after.

PORT ROYAL

Despite the losses at the Isle de Sainte Croix, Champlain and Dugua were determined to carry on and build New France. The explorer persuaded Dugua to return to a site they had seen earlier. Because it was a large enough harbor to fit much of the French navy, Champlain called it Port Royal. The port sat at the delta where the Annapolis River empties into the Bay of Fundy. What is today Nova Scotia sheltered Port Royal from the open sea. This gave it a milder climate than the Isle de Sainte Croix. Champlain and Dugua set to work. They built what would become

With a storehouse for grain, a chapel, and buildings clustered together, Champlain's settlement at Port Royal was home to a hardy band of French colonists until 1607.

the first successful French settlement in the New World. It was also the first European settlement north of Florida. Champlain lived at Port Royal for two years. During that time, he forged alliances with the local Micmac Indians. He also explored and mapped farther down the coast.

MAPPING THE NORTHEAST

Always ready to explore and chart what he found, Champlain used Port Royal as a base. He continued to search for new settlement sites. He cruised down the coastline of what is now Maine to Cape Cod and Plymouth, Massachusetts. As he traveled, he sailed in and out of coves and inlets—what he called ferreting. He drew detailed maps and named the places he saw, like Mount Desert Island. Today it is the home of Acadia National Park. The explorer spent two years at Port Royal, mapping the northeast coast of North America. He made an attempt to follow the shore down as far

Today's Acadia National Park takes its name from the French word for the coastal region of Maine, New Brunswick, and Nova Scotia.

as Florida. Problems with his ship and a battle with the local Nauset tribe stopped him. At first, members of the tribe welcomed the French. But some of Champlain's men helped themselves to the tribe's produce without asking. They also marched around with their weapons at the ready. Champlain quickly decided to return to Port Royal.

FOUNDING QUEBEC

Champlain planned on creating French settlements across the region. This would ensure a prosperous fur trade and a strong, peaceful New France. Dugua shared this vision. He saw that Champlain was given the resources—ships, soldiers, and workers—he needed to carry out this plan. On July 3, 1608, Samuel de Champlain began construction of a new community on the St. Lawrence River. Its name was Habitation de Quebec. Today, it is known as Quebec. The name came from the Algonquin word *kébec*, which meant "where the stream narrows." This refers to the St. Lawrence River. Built around a stockade, the

Samuel de Champlain is known today as the founder of Quebec City. The first settlement on the site dates back to 1608, when he built the Habitation de Quebec.

village housed several cabins, storehouses, and a chapel. The surrounding land was cleared for farming. Another miserable winter nearly wiped out the community. Sixteen of the twenty-four settlers died of scurvy and dysentery. But it was the beginning of the Quebec City we know today.

CHAMPLAIN'S NATIVE ALLIES

Nobody knew hunting and trapping in North America better than the Native Americans. Champlain realized that if the French wanted to dominate the fur trade, he'd need their help. So the explorer built close alliances with the Montagnais and their Algonquin allies, tribes he met along the St. Lawrence. By doing this, though, he was pitted against the powerful Iroquois Confederacy. This nation included an alliance of the Mohawk, Onondaga, Oneida, Seneca, and Cayuga peoples. Champlain promised his new friends that he'd help them defeat their old enemies. To that end,

Allied with the Huron and Algonquin tribes, Champlain had several battles with their enemy the Iroquois. Their first battle in 1609 ended after Champlain fired his arquebus.

he paddled up the Richelieu River with a fleet of war canoes to do battle with the Iroquois. The first skirmish went well. When Champlain fired his booming gun—an arquebus—the Iroquois fled. Two of their chiefs were killed in the skirmish. This incident in 1609 set up more than a century of conflict between the French and the Iroquois.

RULER OF NEW FRANCE

The king of France—not Henry now but Louis XIII—bestowed yet another honor on Champlain. In 1612, he asked the explorer to become master of his domains in North America. Champlain was to serve under a viceroy. This official had no plans to cross the Atlantic, though. That made the explorer the de facto ruler of New France. Champlain is mainly famous as an explorer and mapmaker. But he was also a world-class diplomat. Each trip to the New World required him to amass a great deal of money. He also had to figure out how to run

In 1613, Champlain drew this map of New France, which extended from what's now Quebec Province, in Canada, south past Cape Cod, and all the way west beyond the Great Lakes.

an expedition, collect supplies, find men, and so on. Champlain expertly navigated the king's court and business circles to find the resources he needed. His career spanned two kings, a regent, the reign of a powerful cardinal, and countless French business leaders.

CHARTING NEW TERRITORIES

When he returned to New France in 1613, Champlain set out again to do what he did best—explore and map. He still wanted to find the "northern sea" the Huron people had told him about. Historians believe they were referring to Hudson Bay. His travels took him farther down the Ottawa River into terrain never before charted by Europeans. Later that year, he went back to France and began writing his memoirs. These would later become his famous tome, *Voyages*. He also drew new maps of New France. Champlain was a skilled artist. His work was filled with hundreds of charts and

Published in 1632, Champlain's book was filled with maps and drawings of life in New France, such as this one showing how the Native Americans hunted for deer.

drawings. In this way, he shared with the people of France what it was like to visit New France. *Les Voyages de la Nouvelle France occidentale, dicte Canada, faits par le Sr de Champlain* was published in 1632. It spanned seven hundred pages. The material in it came from the journals he kept during his voyages.

WAR WITH THE IROQUOIS

After his easy initial victory over the Iroquois, Champlain assumed it would be easy to force the tribes off their lands. This would open up more territory for fur trading and French settlements. In 1615, he went to war against the confederacy. He led his Indian allies on an attack on an Onondaga fort on the shores of Lake Huron. The Huron persuaded him to attack, before five hundred reinforcements could arrive. This early move ended in Champlain's defeat. The great explorer was also wounded. He took two arrows to the leg and had to be hauled off the battlefield on the back of a

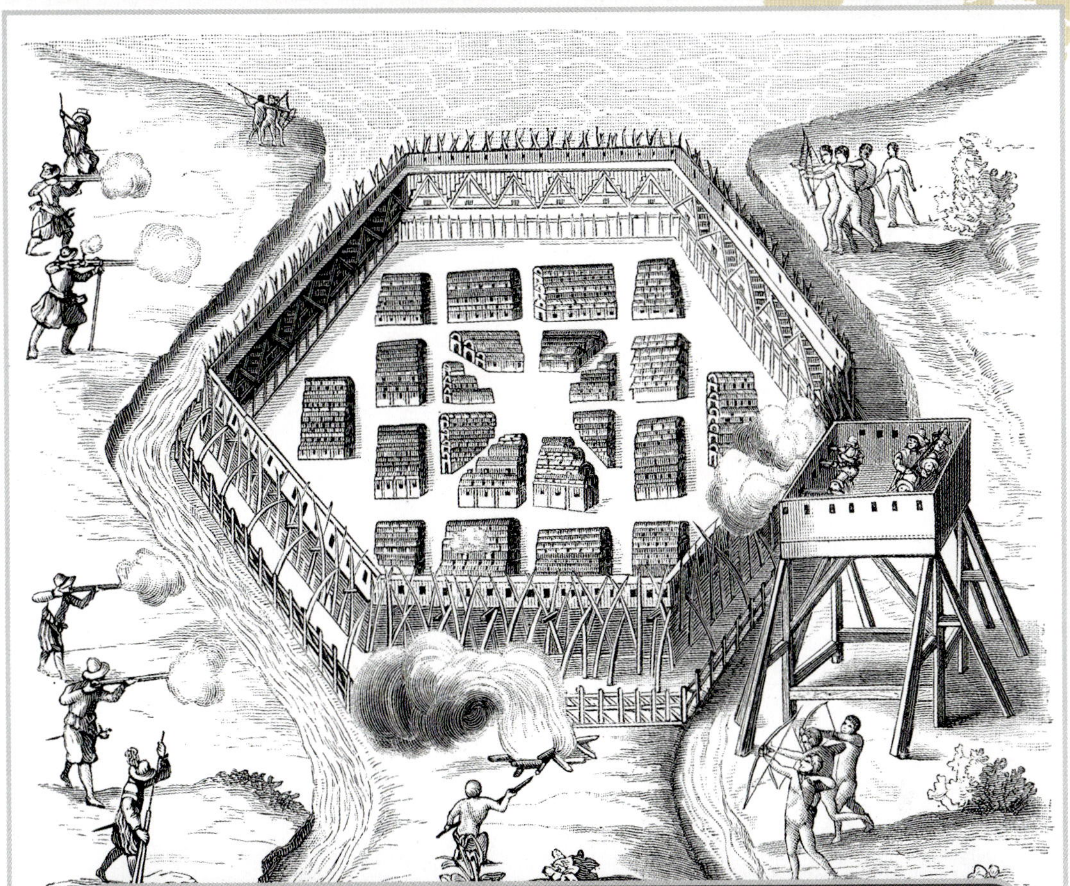

Champlain was wounded in several battles with the Iroquois, including this 1615 attack on an Onondaga fort, which ended in disaster for the French and their allies.

Huron warrior. Champlain had promised the Huron a victory, but he could not keep that promise. The loss strained the relationship between the French and their Native American allies. The Huron insisted that Champlain stay with them to plan another attack. He lived among them for the winter, learning their ways.

ONE LAST LOOK AROUND

Champlain did the last of his explorations of the New World with the Huron. He traveled even farther down the Ottawa River. There, he came upon another massive freshwater body. He called it Lac Attigouautan—today it's known as Lake Huron. With the explorer's help, the French established a route to expand the fur trade greatly. It followed the Ottawa to Georgian Bay on Lake Huron.

By 1620, when he was forty-six years old, Samuel de Champlain hung up his traveling boots. He became too busy governing and building settlements to go venturing off into the uncharted wilderness. Pressing matters in

Samuel de Champlain literally put Lake Huron on the map, and he helped the French expand their fur trade beyond it, resulting in massive growth for the industry.

the construction of New France consumed his attention. These included negotiating a peace treaty with his old enemies the Iroquois and striking up a new fur-trading partnership. This partnership involved Armand Jean du Plessis, Cardinal-Duke of Richelieu, an ambitious clergyman who was amassing power back in France.

THE WALLS GO UP

Quebec is the only remaining fortified city north of Mexico with walls still standing. Champlain laid the first stones for its famous walls on May 6, 1624. As early as 1618, the great cartographer had drawn plans for the city he envisioned at Quebec. He called it Ludovica, in honor of King Louis XIII. That dream never came to life. But the explorer never gave up on the site. He spent years helping to construct the foundations for the city. In the 1620s, he began building the city's famous ramparts, towering, castle-like walls, to defend it from attack. He also began to construct what is known today as the Upper

Built atop soaring cliffs on a bend in the mighty St. Lawrence River, Quebec City rose from the small fort Champlain built there in 1608.

Town. With Champlain's guidance, Quebec became the hub of the French fur trade. This made Quebec a small but extremely valuable outpost perched above the St. Lawrence River. By 1627, it had a population of more than one hundred people.

FRANCE VERSUS ENGLAND

In 1628, the old European nemesis of the French, the English, began to move in on their territory in the New World. Across the Atlantic, the bitter rivals were once again at war. By then, the English had colonized Massachusetts Bay and Virginia. They were also expanding north into what is now Maine. But the presence of the French impeded their growth. So the English turned their attention on Quebec, demanding that the settlement be turned over to them. Champlain refused, and the English set up a blockade. This prevented the French from reaching Quebec with supplies. It worked.

Champlain held out as long as he could against an English blockade that starved Quebec, but eventually he was forced to surrender the colony to the English in 1629.

Quebec began to starve. Champlain had little in the way of ammunition and was ultimately forced to surrender Quebec. He was taken as a prisoner back to England. But when the ship he was held captive on arrived in Plymouth, England, in October 1629, the war between England and France was over.

BUILDING ANEW

Three years later, Champlain was back in Quebec. A treaty with England returned Quebec to the French. Champlain resumed his work governing the French colonies in the New World. When he arrived at Quebec, Champlain discovered that the English had decimated the village. Years of hard work were destroyed. But he and his colonists turned right to rebuilding. They modeled the community after a traditional French *ville*, or city. Champlain reported to Cardinal Richelieu that by 1634 they had erected new fortifications on the site of the old Quebec. They were also busy building two

The French lived in harmony with many native tribes during the early days of New France.

more communities farther upriver. When the Huron heard that their old friend had come back, they visited Quebec in hundreds of large canoes. They told Champlain that trouble was once again brewing with the Iroquois. The English had been encouraging the confederacy to betray its peace treaty with the French.

END OF AN EXPLORER

The Father of New France suffered a severe stroke in October 1635. The Jesuits of Quebec cared for him. On Christmas Day of that year, he died. He never saw his dream of a peaceful and prosperous New France come to fruition. Still, Samuel de Champlain left behind a lasting legacy. His exploration—and his maps—opened up huge swaths of the North American continent to further explorers and mapmakers. The French fur trade would become a huge moneymaker. Quebec City, born from French influence, would rise to become a beautiful and important city. And French

The great explorer Samuel de Champlain is honored here at Champlain Memorial Lighthouse at Crown Point, New York, where he is shown with a French voyageur and a Huron guide.

culture would have a lasting impact on North America. Places like New Orleans, where many Acadians migrated and became Cajuns, still have strong French ties. French building styles can be seen from Mississippi and Alabama to Michigan and Illinois. Today, French is the second-most-spoken language in Louisiana and in northern New England. Champlain's New France lives on.

GLOSSARY

Acadia The name that the French gave to the New World, specifically the northeast of North America, where Maine and the Canadian Maritimes are today.

Bay of Fundy A great body of water between the Maine coast and Nova Scotia.

cartographer Someone who makes maps.

colony A settlement or area ruled by another country.

geographer A person who studies the earth, its features, and the various populations on the planet.

Huron A native people from the Great Lakes area.

Iroquois A confederacy of Indian tribes in the Great Lakes area that became allies of the English.

Jesuit A member of an order of Catholic priests known for missionary work.

Montagnais A native people of Quebec.

Northwest Passage The route to the Far East through North America that European explorers thought they would find.

scurvy A sickness caused by lack of vitamin C, common to sailors.

Sieur An honorary title meaning "sir" or "sire."

St. Lawrence River The massive waterway that connects the Great Lakes to the Atlantic Ocean, in the northeast of North America.

stockade A tall wooden fence built as a fortification.

viceroy One who rules a region or country in the name of the king.

FOR MORE INFORMATION

Canadian Museum of History
100 Laurier Street
Gatineau, QC K1A 0M8
Canada
(819) 776-7000
Website: http://www.historymuseum.ca
The Canadian Museum of History in Gatineau is home to a wealth of information about Samuel de Champlain, the fur trade, Jacques Cartier, the Sieur de Mons, and more.

The Fur Trade at Lachine National Historic Site
1255 Saint-Joseph Boulevard
Lachine Borough
Montréal, QC H8S 2M2
Canada
(514) 637-7433
Website: http://www.pc.gc.ca/eng/lhn-nhs/qc/lachine/index.aspx
Imagine what it was like to be a French voyageur, trading for furs with the natives, at this Canadian historic site.

National Park Service Saint Croix Island Historic Site
PO Box 247
Calais, ME 04619
(207) 454-3871
Website: http://www.nps.gov/sacr/index.htm

The National Park Service (NPS) runs this international historic site at St. Croix Island jointly with Parks Canada. A small park with interpretive displays, it gives visitors a flavor of what it was like to be there in the winter of 1604 with Samuel de Champlain and the Sieur de Mons.

Quebec City Tourism
Quebec/Borough of La Cité-Limoilou (Vieux-Quebec)
12, rue Sainte-Anne
Quebec, QC G1R 3X2
(877) BONJOUR (1-877-266-5687)
Website: http://www.quebecregion.com/en
Learn more about Quebec City and its history. Find information on a variety of excellent museums that celebrate the history of New France. Or plan a visit!

Websites

Because of the changing nature of internet links, Rosen Publishing has developed an online list of websites related to the subject of this book. This site is updated regularly. Please use this link to access the list:

http://www.rosenlinks.com/SEC/champ

FOR FURTHER READING

Bedard, Eric. *History of Quebec for Dummies*. Mississauga, ON: John Wiley and Sons, Canada, 2013.

Johnston, Lissa. *A Brief Political and Geographic History of North America: Where Are New France, New Netherland, and New Sweden?* Newark, DE: Mitchell Lane Publishers, 2007.

Kalman, Bobbie. *Life in a Longhouse Village*. St. Catherines, ON: Crabtree Publishing, 2001.

Legare, Francine. *Samuel de Champlain*. Translated by Johnathan Kaplansky. Toronto, ON: Dundurn Press, 2004.

Mooney, Carla, and Tom Casteel. *Explorers of the New World: Discover the Golden Age of Exploration with 22 Projects.* White River Junction, VT: Nomad Press, 2011.

Morganelli, Adrianna. *Samuel de Champlain: From New France to Cape Cod*. St. Catherines, ON: Crabtree Publishing, 2006.

O'Brien, Cynthia. *Explore with Samuel de Champlain*. St. Catherines, ON: Crabtree Publishing, 2014.

Pelleschi, Andrea. *Samuel de Champlain*. New York, NY: PowerKids Press, 2013.

Peterson, Cris. *Birchbark Brigade: A Fur Trade History*. Honesdale, PA: Calkins Creek, 2009.

BIBLIOGRAPHY

American Treasures of the Library of Congress. Samuel de Champlain's 1607 Map. Retrieved April 10, 2016. https://www.loc.gov/exhibits/treasures/trr009.html.

Boswell, Randy. "Baptism Record that Solved Mystery of Samuel de Champlain's Birth Arrives in Canada for 400th Anniversary Exhibit." O Canada.com. May 17, 2013. http://o.canada.com/news/baptism-record-that-solved-mystery-of-champlains-birth-arrives-in-canada-for-400th-anniversary-exhibit.

Canadian Museum of History. Virtual Museum of New France: The Explorers: Samuel de Champlain 1604–1616. Retrieved April 5, 2016. http://www.historymuseum.ca/virtual-museum-of-new-france/the-explorers/samuel-de-champlain-1604-1616.

Champlain, Samuel de, and William Lawson Grant. *Voyages of Samuel de Champlain: 1604-1618*. New York, NY: Charles Scribner's Sons, 1907.

Fisher, David Hackett. *Champlain's Dream*. New York, NY: Simon and Schuster, 2008.

Morganelli, Adrianna. *Samuel de Champlain: From New France to Cape Cod*. St. Catherines, ON: Crabtree Publishing, 2006.

National Park Service. Saint Croix Island International Historic Site. Retrieved April 5, 2016. https://www.nps.gov/sacr/index.htm.

INDEX

About the Author

Andrew Vietze loves to explore history! He's the author of ten books, including the number-one Amazon best seller in US history *Boon Island*, the award-winning biography *Becoming Teddy Roosevelt*, and Rosen's *Kublai Khan: Emperor of China*. A frequent visitor to Quebec City, he lives in Maine not far from Acadia National Park.

Photo Credits

Cover, p. 29 DEA Picture Library/De Agostini/Getty Images; cover, interior pages, back cover (map) Designer things/Shutterstock.com; cover, pp. 1, 3 (scroll) © iStockphoto.com/HADAV; cover, interior pages (compass) Happy Art/Shutterstock.com; pp. 5, 31 Photos.com /Thinkstock; p. 7 Hemera Technologies/Photos.com/Thinkstock; p. 9 Dorling Kindersley/Thinkstock; p. 11 © iStockphoto.com/ZU_09; p. 13 Royal Commonwealth Society, London, UK/Bridgeman Images; p. 15 Massimiliano Pieraccini/Shutterstock.com; p. 17 GeorgiosArt/ iStock/Thinkstock.com; p. 19 Verena Matthew/Shutterstock.com; p. 21 Jon Bilous/Shutterstock.com; p. 23 © North Wind Picture Archives/The Image Works; p. 25 © iStockphoto.com/Steven Wynn; pp. 27, 35 © North Wind Picture Archives/Alamy Stock Photo; p. 33 MarkauMark/Shutterstock.com; p. 37 Private Collection/ © Look and Learn/Elgar Collection/Bridgeman Images; p. 39 Private Collection/© Look and Learn/Bridgeman Images; p. 41 © Syracuse Newspapers/D Lassman/The Image Works.

Designer: Nicole Russo; Editor and Photo Researcher: Xina Uhl